I0766463

Dedicated to
My first grandson, the new love of my life,
Yisrael Avraham (Sruly), who brings so much joy and love to me, to my family,
and to everyone he meets;
And to my future grandchildren and to all the children around the world
May you always recognize how precious you truly are

My precious family, whose love and support is invaluable:

My daughter, Chana Leah
My son and daughter, Yechezkel and Menuchah Rochel
My husband Dovid, my soul partner, who supports all my projects in every way possible

Special Thanks to
Gayle Dancer, for her creative assistance that brought this book to life and to completion.
Reva S. Baer, as ever, for her editorial contributions and so much else
Yehudit Wider and family, especially Ariella, for their continual generosity

Special thanks to the artist, Sarah Chyrek, for doing such a fantastic job, bringing this
book to life, and being so accommodating and easy to work with. Your artwork is truly
beautiful and brilliant!

Special thanks to Lea Kron for her dedicated assistance with graphic design and editing,
content editing, and uploading books to Amazon

Much appreciation to all my team members, my devoted and dedicated partners in
bringing more Torah to the world--
it is such a pleasure to work with you!

Prince Chaim thought that the King, his father, was the
kindest, most wonderful person he knew.

He wanted to be just like him, and hoped that he would
learn to lead with justice and kindness, as the King did.

The prince had many Rebbis and tutors to help him on
his quest to become like his father. During lessons, Prince
Chaim would look out the window and daydream.

He would often have to be gently brought back from his daydreams by his teachers. "Chaim," they would say, "to learn properly, you need to focus on what is in front of you, not on what is outside."

Among the many subjects he was taught was chesed, kindness. People were always so kind to him that Prince Chaim grew very excited with the idea of helping others.

He knew just where to start. The royal kitchen was one of his favorite places in the King's palace.

One day, after classes ended, Prince
Chaim went quickly down the stairs
that led to the kitchen and asked to
speak to the royal baker.

The royal baker smiled at the prince.
"Your Highness, what can I do for you?" he asked.
Prince Chaim smiled back and replied,
"Thank you for asking. But actually, I'm here to ask
if you need any help."

The baker looked at the prince, remembering what
an active personality he was.
"Well, I could use some help with rolling out the
dough for the dessert at this Shabbos evening's
meal," the baker said heartily.
"Come along, I'll show you what to do." The prince
gladly followed the baker.

The royal baker guided Prince Chaim to a large
table where large bowls of dough were resting. The
baker took one bowl and gave the prince another
one, and he began to demonstrate how to shape and
roll the dough. The prince found it to be very
interesting and fun. He put a lot of effort and
enthusiasm into copying the royal baker's
movements as best he could.

As Prince Chaim stretched out his arms, preparing to roll the dough so thin, he accidentally knocked a large metal bowl of flour off the table. Suddenly, the kitchen was filled with a tremendous clanging noise, and the prince, the baker, and everything around them was covered in a soft, snow-colored mess.

Under the white film, the baker's face had turned an interesting shade of red.

He took a deep breath, actually, several deep breaths, and then calmly told the prince, "Perhaps I should have prepared our work area better. Due to circumstances, however, I think it would be best, Prince Chaim, if you were to leave the kitchen until this is cleaned up."

"I'm sorry!" Prince Chaim exclaimed. "I'll help you clean it up!"

"No, thank you, that will not be necessary. Leaving the kitchen—that is necessary."

Prince Chaim left the kitchen, his eyes downcast. As he walked through the palace hallways, leaving a white flour trail behind him, Prince Chaim thought, "My father would have performed this act of chesed perfectly. Why couldn't I also do this mitzvah perfectly?"

Prince Chaim kept going over the "flour incident" in his head, feeling worse and worse every minute.

He thought that his father had certainly been told about it. He felt so ashamed that when he came to his father's study he quietly crept past it. Prince Chaim could not bear to see his father's disappointment.

He walked dejectedly out of the palace, into the royal garden, and threw himself down on the grass by the beautiful fish pond. He stared at his sorrowful reflection in the water.

Prince Chaim was startled to hear a voice say,
"Your Highness, whatever is the matter?"
"Huh? Who is that?" The prince turned around
and saw Berel, the royal gardener, looking at him
with concern.

"Oh, hello, Berel. Well…," Prince Chaim was
embarrassed to discuss his troubles, but he knew
that Berel the gardener was a very wise man. Maybe
Berel would have some good advice. Prince Chaim
decided to confide in him.

"You see," the prince began, "my father is perfect
and wonderful. He does so much chesed and helps
so many people. But I can't even manage to roll out
dough for my own dessert without making a huge,
noisy mess. I especially want to perform mitzvos
very well, but it looks like I'm doing just the
opposite. It looks like I'm no help to anyone; I just
mess up all the time."

Berel could well imagine how the royal kitchen must
have looked. Yet, Berel had always enjoyed Prince
Chaim's charm and good cheer, and he had been
noticing lately that the young prince did not seem to
be his usual happy self. He took the prince's
statements very seriously.

"Your Highness," Berel said, "we are taught in the Torah that the performance of mitzvos takes practice, just like learning to read or playing a musical instrument.

Do you think that my work as a gardener is over when I plant the seeds into the ground?

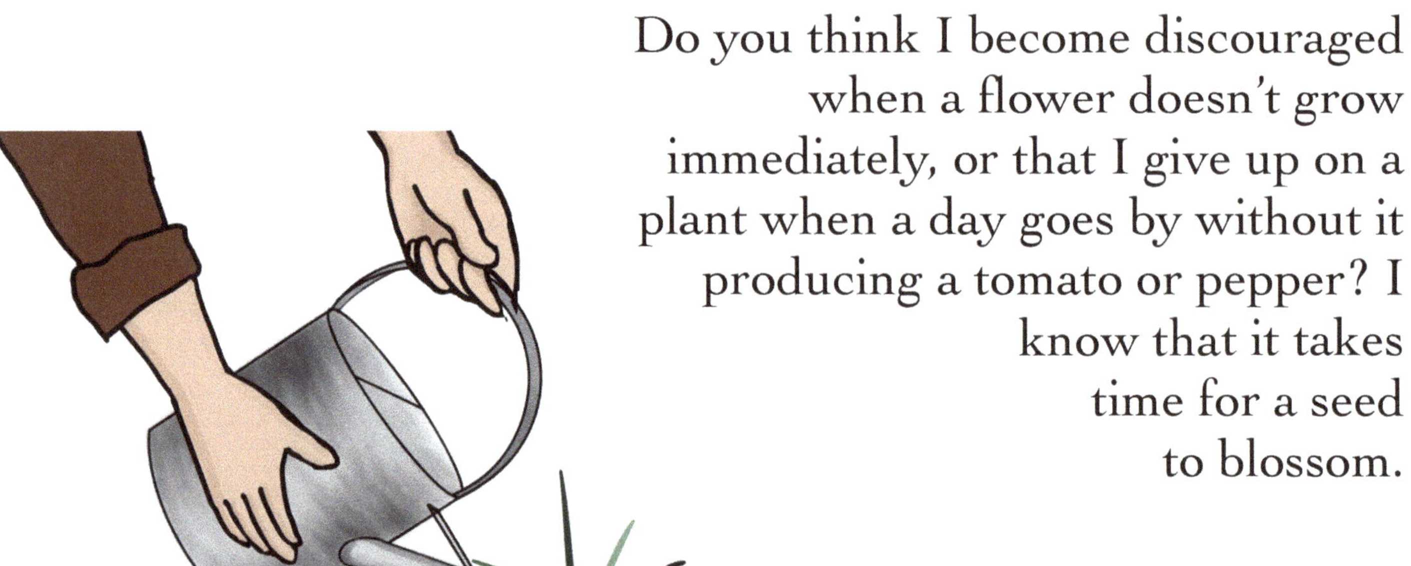

Do you think I become discouraged when a flower doesn't grow immediately, or that I give up on a plant when a day goes by without it producing a tomato or pepper? I know that it takes time for a seed to blossom.

My job is to keep watering the seeds and tending
to the plants. And as you see before you, because
with G-d's help, I don't give up, seeds and dirt
turn into a beautiful garden!"

"Hmmm. Yes, you have a point," Prince Chaim responded with a sigh, "but it is very hard for me to believe that I can ever learn how to do mitzvos well.

You see, my father, my mother, and my teachers all speak to me about giving to others who have less than I do, but in all honesty, how can I? What can I give anyone? Whatever I try is likely to end in disaster if I'm involved," the prince said sullenly.

Berel thought for a moment and then gently said, "I hear you. I understand better than you can imagine. I used to feel the same way."

"Really?" Prince Chaim questioned in disbelief. "Yes, I really did! As I got older, though, I started studying the deep secrets of the Torah. I learned that everyone has a cheilek Elokai mema'al, a part of G-dliness inside of us. I began to have a better understanding of how holy I am. I began to realize that my self-worth is 100% based on the simple fact that I exist and am G-d's masterpiece! You, my dear Prince Chaim, are also G-d's masterpiece! You are not judged by the mistakes that you have made but by the soul inside you, that is like G-d's diamond on display."

צדקה

The prince's eyes widened. "Wow!"

"Your parents, the King and Queen, love you very much," Berel continued. "I have known you since you were born, and I remember all about the great things you have done. Now, you should try to remember those things, too. Why, I remember when you were just four years old and you broke down and cried when you thought that someone was far away from Hashem. What four-year-old does that?"
"Really?" the prince asked, "I cried about that?"

"Yes, you really broke down in sobbing tears, you felt so sad for Hashem and for that person. And how about when you would go to the army base and shake lulav and esrog with the soldiers with such joy, when you were not even three! That was a real chesed."

Berel pointed his spade in the air. "I remember those kind acts, and many more. Dear precious Prince Chaim, remember this well: your mistakes do not define you! You need to look at the whole of you."

A beautiful smile appeared on Prince Chaim's face. His eyes shone with hope and faith. "Oh, thank you, Berel, you've really made me feel so much better," the prince said with sincerity.

"Don't thank me," the gardener replied. "I need to thank you, for giving me the opportunity of doing the mitzvah of cheering someone up!" Berel stood still.

"You know what? Come to think about cheering someone up—let's work together to cheer someone up. I have an idea, my dear Prince! You surely are needed, as I am very busy tending to the palace grounds and gardens."

Prince Chaim was standing up now to listen more closely to Berel. "It is almost Chanukah, and I just heard of a family that does not have oil and a menorah to light. That seems so sad. Maybe this is a mitzvah that you, Your Highness, can do. It would please Hashem, your parents, and yourself, since you would be doing something for someone else."

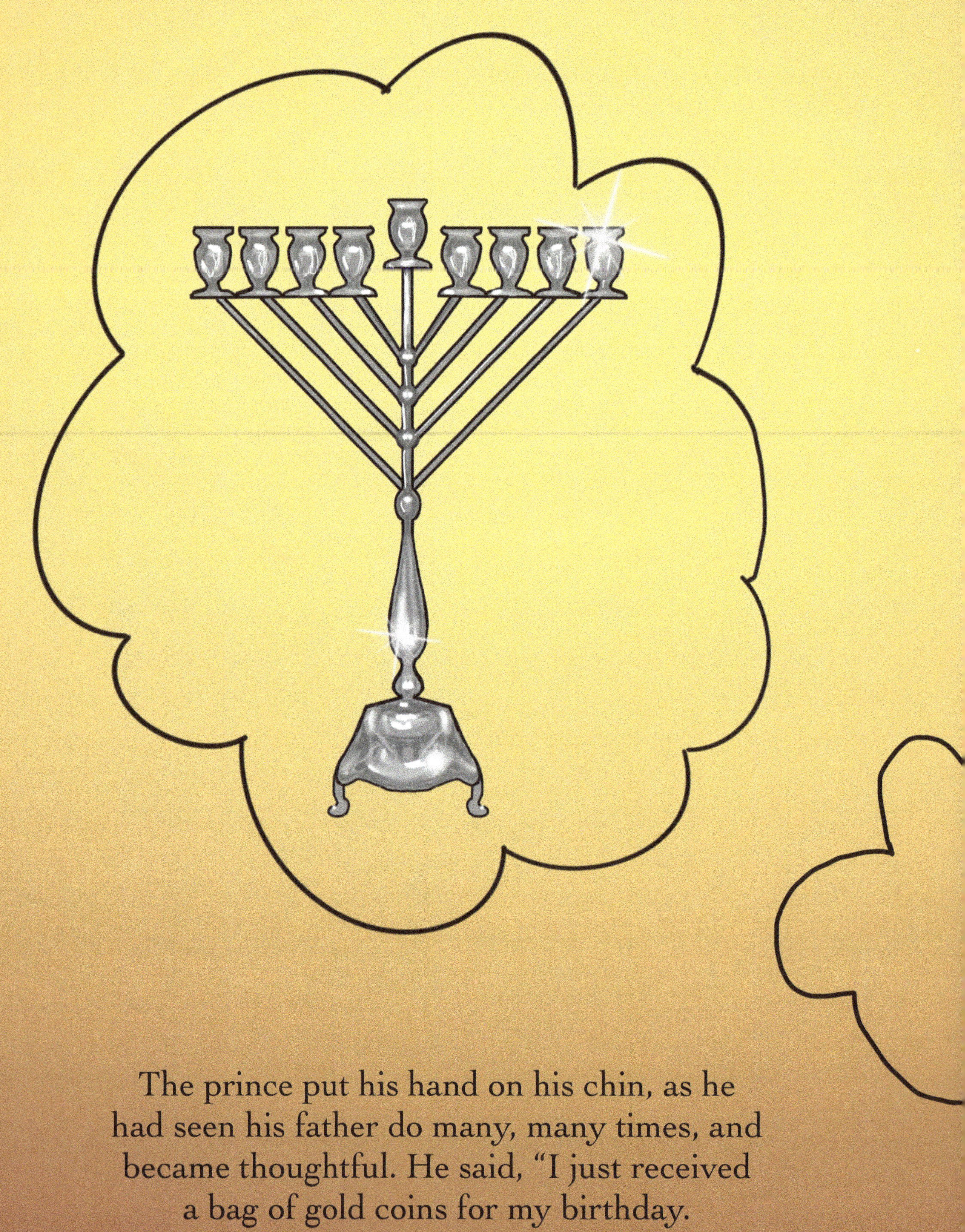

The prince put his hand on his chin, as he
had seen his father do many, many times, and
became thoughtful. He said, "I just received
a bag of gold coins for my birthday.

I will use it to buy a menorah from
Simchah the royal silversmith. I will buy
them the most beautiful one he has, with
crystal cups to hold the oil, so they can
light it and be happy on Chanukah."
The prince, for the first time in a very
long time, grinned broadly.

"Thank you again, Berel. I want to do this
right away! I'll be back soon, I hope." He
shook the gardener's hand, and then ran
to his royal chamber. He quickly took his
money and ran to complete his mission.

Prince Chaim knocked on the door of the royal silversmith's workshop. "Welcome, your Highness," Simchah the silversmith greeted him.
"To what do I owe the honor of this royal visit?"

"Reb Simchah, I'm super excited to be doing a very special mitzvah!" Prince Chaim replied. "I want the most beautiful menorah you have, and I am going to pay for it with my own money."

After Reb Simchah heard Prince Chaim's plan, he was so impressed that he said, "I want to be part of this mitzvah, too. Please accept these dreidels and some Chanukah gelt coins for the family."

Prince Chaim thanked the silversmith, then went to his next stop, the royal kitchen. Prince Chaim politely asked the royal chef if he could please have a bottle of oil.

"Of course, Prince Chaim," the chef replied. In his excitement, the prince told the royal chef his plan. The royal chef exclaimed, "I also want to be part of this mitzvah!"

In addition to the large bottle of olive oil, the chef prepared a beautiful platter of Chanukah doughnuts filled with fresh strawberry jam and another large platter of delicious potato latkes.

Finally, Prince Chaim returned to the garden. He ran up to Berel the gardener and said, "Berel, I feel great! Not only did I get something for the family, but others helped as well! Now, let's go. Where does this family live?"

Berel answered, "It would be my honor to escort you to them, but of course I must ask your father the King for permission to do so, Your Highness."

Together they went to the King to ask permission. Prince Chaim's father was very impressed by his son's wonderful news. "I also want to participate in this mitzvah!" he exclaimed. The King added a significant amount of gold coins into the gift basket. "I would like to see the family myself," the King said.

So the King, the Prince, and the royal gardener entered the royal carriage and made their way to the village where the poor family lived.

When they arrived at the little house, Prince Chaim knocked on the door. The family was very surprised to see their royal visitors, but warmly welcomed them into their home. The prince presented the family with their gifts. The father and mother watched as the children unwrapped them.

When they saw the golden menorah, the oil, the golden coins, the dreidels, and the Chanukah delicacies, the family laughed in delight. The children started to dance while singing, "We get to do a mitzvah, we get to do a mitzvah!"

The grateful father said, "We could not be happier, Your Highness; I don't know how you knew that we needed a menorah! We could not afford to purchase a new one. Thank you so, so much, for everything."

The children looked at the menorah, and then at Prince Chaim.

"Please, Your Highness, it's getting dark—please stay and light the first flame with us! That would make our mitzvah even more special!"

Prince Chaim looked at his father, the King. "It is your mitzvah, and your decision, my son," said the King.

"I realize it will delay the royal menorah lighting, Father, but I would like to stay. I think it would truly make us all happy to see the mitzvah being performed."

The King smiled at his son, and Prince Chaim beamed at the children.

"Yay! Let's set it up right away!" They made the blessings and lit the flame, and Prince Chaim, the King, and Berel joined in singing Chanukah songs. The oldest boy smiled shyly at Prince Chaim. "I wish I could do chesed like you do, some day."

"You can do it now!" Prince Chaim exclaimed. "Just look around and think of something that would make someone else happy, and do what you can to make it happen."

"I know!" The boy whispered, "I'm going to clean up after we eat, so my mother won't have to!"

"Great idea!" the Prince cheered. "Keep it up!" He shook the boy's hand.

"We have to go now and light our menorah with my mother, too."

The prince said a cheerful goodbye to the family and got back into the carriage with the King and Berel. Prince Chaim could hardly wait to reach the palace again. He wanted to tell his mother all about his wonderful experience.

"I am very proud of you, my son," the King told
Prince Chaim, "and I know that your mother will be,
too. And I believe Berel is as well."

"Yes, I am indeed, Your Majesty," the gardener
agreed. Both men smiled at Prince Chaim.
"Do you know why we kindle the Chanukah lights by
a door or a window, my son?" the King asked.

Prince Chaim looked thoughtful. "It is so that we can
share our light with others," the King went on. "The
light of the menorah, the light of the Torah, the light
of chesed, should spread beyond our own courtyard,
to whoever is in need."

The King patted Prince Chaim's shoulder. "You are
becoming quite a lamplighter, my boy. May you
continue your chesed always."

The Queen was indeed very pleased that Prince Chaim had thought about someone else's happiness before his own. When she heard how Prince Chaim had used his own money to buy the menorah, and had inspired others to be a part of the mitzvah, she gave her son a great big hug.

From that day on, Prince Chaim took to heart what the gardener had taught him. Prince Chaim felt happy and confident, and in time, he became a true leader of his people, just like his father the King.

CHILDREN'S BOOKS BY MIRIAM YERUSHALMI

Available on Amazon.com
and on Yournewheights.org

Also available in Hebrew & Yiddish

Also available in Hebrew & Yiddish

Also available in Hebrew & Yiddish

Also available in Yiddish

Also available in Yiddish

Also available in Yiddish

Also available in Yiddish

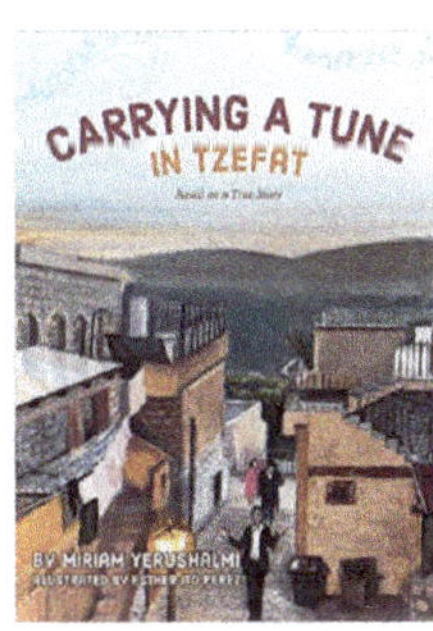

Also available in Yiddish

Also available in Yiddish

Also available in Yiddish

Also available in Spanish

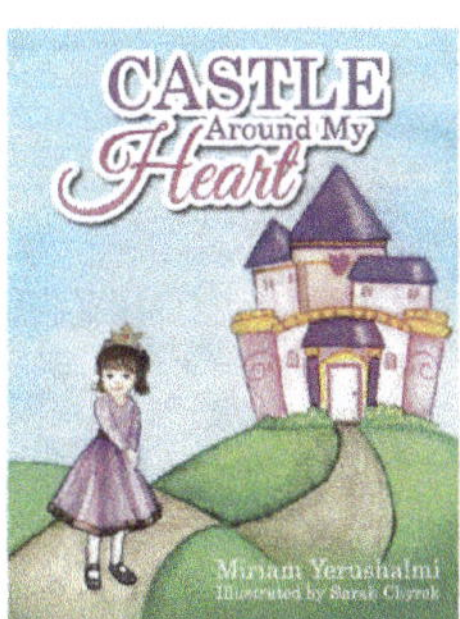

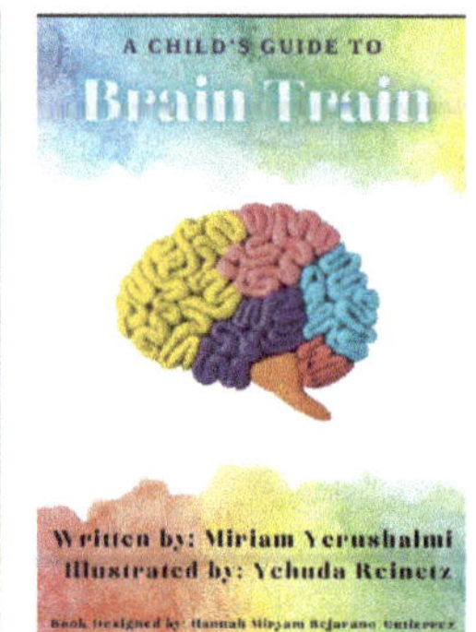

ADULT BOOKS BY MIRIAM YERUSHALMI

Available on Amazon.com
and on Yournewheights.com

COMING SOON:

The Temple Within
Reaching New Heights Through Healthier Cooking
Reaching New Heights Through Living Tanya

ABOUT THE AUTHOR

Miriam Yerushalmi has an MA degree in Psychology and
Marriage and Family Counseling. She has worked extensively
with children for over 40 years, creating brain training programs
to teach self-regulation through drama, dance and the arts.